Catch that thief!

"Some evil thief stole my hoodie. I have an idea. I'll hire the three of you to find my hoodie!" Nadine said suddenly. "How long do you think it will take?"

Nancy glanced at George and Bess, who both nodded yes. "We'll accept your case," she said.

"If you want to find your hoodie fast, Nadine, then you need to hire *real* detectives," someone said.

Nancy, George, Bess, and Nadine all looked around to see who had spoken. Deirdre was standing behind them on the sidewalk, along with Madison and Kendra.

"Real detectives? What are you talking about?" Nadine asked Deirdre curiously.

"I'm taking about me, Madison, and Kendra. We're the Klue Krew, and you should hire us instead of these inexperienced amateurs," Deirdre said, pointing to Nancy, George, and Bess.

Join the CLUE CREW
& solve these other cases!

NANCY DREW
AND THE CLUE CREW ®

#21

Double Take

BY CAROLYN KEENE

ILLUSTRATED BY MACKY PAMINTUAN

SCHOLASTIC INC.
New York Toronto London Auckland
Sydney Mexico City New Delhi Hong Kong

ISBN 978-0-545-28443-1

12 11 10 9 8 7 6 5 4 3 2 1   10 11 12 13 14 15/0

Printed in the U.S.A.   75

First Scholastic printing, September 2010

Designed by Lisa Vega
The text of this book was set in ITC Stone Informal.

CONTENTS

Double Take

ChAPTER ONE

Fashion Show and Tell

"Check out my new jeans," Deidre Shannon said. She stood up and twirled around like a fashion model.

Nancy Drew glanced at Deirdre's jeans. The paint flecks were a mixture of white and pale pink and baby blue.

"Did you spill paint on them in art class?" Bess Marvin asked Deirdre curiously.

Deirdre rolled her eyes. "Uh, no. They came this way. And they're *way* more expensive than jeans that *aren't* splattered with paint." She pointed to the ones Nancy was wearing. "You know—like those?"

Nancy tried to hide her smile. Typical Deirdre! She always liked to brag that she had the best or the fanciest stuff.

Nancy and Bess were eating lunch in the school cafeteria with George Fayne. Deirdre was at the next table, along with Madison Foley and Kendra Jackson. The air was filled with the yummy smells of today's specials: chili, chicken nuggets, and Tater Tots.

"I guess I could just spill some paint on my jeans," George piped up as she nibbled on a chicken nugget. "Then everyone would think I had super-cool jeans like yours, Deirdre."

"Ha ha, *Georgia*," Deirdre said, using George's full name. George made a face at Deirdre. She didn't like being called Georgia.

Nancy, George, and Bess were best friends. George and Bess were also cousins, although it wasn't always easy for people to tell. George had brown hair and brown eyes, while Bess had blond hair and blue eyes. George was into sports, while Bess loved fashion.

"Well, you're not the only one with new clothes, Deirdre," Bess said. She leaned back in her chair and kicked up her feet. "Check out my new boots!"

"Cool red boots," Madison remarked as she popped a Tater Tot into her mouth. Deirdre glared at Madison. "I mean . . . they're okay . . . I guess," Madison revised quickly.

"Actually, they're magenta," Bess corrected Madison. "Magenta is like red mixed with purple."

"And speaking of purple . . . check out my new headband," Nancy said, touching her hair. "I got it at the mall last weekend."

"Headbands are so last week," Deirdre said. "Right, Kendra?"

"Huh?" Kendra said, looking startled. "Uh, right, Deirdre. Whatever you say."

Just then, Nadine Nardo walked up to the girls, carrying a tray. "Are you guys talking about clothes?" she said excitedly. "Because guess what? You'll never believe it!"

"What is it, Nadine?" Deirdre said. She faked a yawn.

Nadine set her tray down on Nancy's table. "I took it off before lunch period because I didn't want to spill anything on it," she explained. She pulled something out of her backpack and slipped it on. "Ta-da!" she cried out. She threw her arms out wide and blew air kisses, like a celebrity.

Nadine was wearing a brand-new pink hoodie. But it wasn't just a regular hoodie. There was a special heart design on the back of it, made of silver sequins. In the center of the heart were some words, also in silver. It looked like someone's autograph.

Nancy squinted. The name was Lila . . . or Lola . . .

Bess gasped. "Oh my gosh! Is that the new Lula Rappaport hoodie, Nadine?"

Nadine beamed proudly. "Isn't it awesome?"

"You mean Lula Rappaport, the actress?" Madison gushed. "I read an article in *Teen Style* magazine that she just started designing clothes. I can't believe you have one of her hoodies, Nadine."

Deirdre glared at Madison again. Madison turned bright red.

"Where did you even buy that, Nadine?" Kendra asked her. "Aren't those hoodies really hard to get?"

"My aunt Chloe got it for me for my birthday," Nadine replied. "Aunt Chloe is a friend of a friend of a friend of Lula Rappaport's publicist."

"Publi-what?" George said.

"Publicist," Deirdre said. "Publicists work for the stars. They make sure they get their names in magazines and stuff." She flipped her dark hair over her shoulders. "I know because my dad deals with stars all the time, for his job. He's way more important than your aunt Whoever, Nadine."

Deirdre's father was the publisher of the local newspaper, the *River Heights Bugle*. Nancy wasn't sure if Deirdre was exaggerating about him dealing with stars "all the time." Probably, knowing Deirdre.

"In fact, Daddy is getting me the exact same Lula Rappaport hoodie right this second," Deirdre went on, studying her nails. "He's also getting me some other stuff from Lula's new fashion line. Like her new pink velvet boots. They're way cooler than your majento boots, Bess."

Bess frowned. "They're magent-*a*!"

Nadine was about to say something. But a voice interrupted her.

"Hey, Nadine. New outfit?"

All the girls turned in the direction of the voice. Antonio Elefano was walking toward them, carrying a tray. Nancy could see steam rising from a bowl of flaming-red chili and about twenty little packages of crackers.

Antonio was a boy in Nancy's third-grade class. He was famous for pulling pranks and causing trouble. He was also famous for taking stuff that didn't belong to him—like extra packages of crackers, when the cafeteria lady wasn't looking.

Nadine smiled uncertainly at Antonio. "Um . . . yeah. It's my new Lula Rappaport hoodie."

"It's pretty awesome," Antonio said with a mischievous grin. "Can I try it on? Just kidding. Oops!"

Antonio tripped, losing his balance right in

front of Nadine. His backpack slipped off his shoulders. His tray began tipping.

Nancy and the other girls gasped in horror. In about two seconds, Antonio's bowl of flaming-red chili would spill all over Nadine's brand-new hoodie!

ChaPTER TWo

Missing!

Nadine screamed. Her new pink hoodie was about to get sprayed with Antonio's chili!

But at the very last second, Antonio miraculously regained his balance and stood up straight. He saw the look of fear on Nadine's face and started cracking up.

"I fooled you, didn't I?" he said, setting his tray down on Nancy's table with a loud *thunk*.

Nadine gasped. "You mean you were just *pretending* to trip?"

"Ha-ha," Antonio crowed.

"That is so mean," Bess scolded him. "You're going to get into big trouble, Antonio!"

Antonio smirked. "For what? For *not* spilling

chili all over Nadine's new pink thing? I don't think so."

Nancy glanced down at the floor. During Antonio's pretend-tripping incident, his backpack had slipped off his shoulders. His stuff was all over the floor, including his pencils, pens, notebooks, and comic books. There was some math homework with lots of red marks on it, too—and a spelling test, also with red marks.

Nancy bent down to pick up the spelling test, which was right next to her feet. But Antonio swooped down and grabbed it before she could.

"That's mine," he said huffily. He stuffed the spelling test and the rest of his belongings into his backpack. Then he picked up his tray. "Later, losers," he called over his shoulder.

"He is so evil," George said after Antonio had gone.

"Super evil," Bess echoed.

"Super-super evil," Nadine agreed. She took off her hoodie hastily and put it back inside her backpack. "I'm keeping it in there for the rest of the day, away from Antonio and his flying bowls of chili. That was *way* too close."

"Last one dressed is a rotten egg!" someone shouted. A wave of girls ran into the girls' locker room, screaming and laughing.

"No running!" the gym teacher, Mr. Wilson, called out. "Everyone, please walk!"

Nancy, Bess, George, and all the other girls slowed down as they squeezed through the doorway. Gym class was over, and it was the end of the day. They had had fun playing dodgeball outside in the warm sun. Now it was time to get changed and go home.

Inside the locker room, all the girls rushed to their lockers. Things were kind of a mess, though. There were clothes strewn all over the floor from before class, when everyone had been in a huge hurry to get changed for gym.

Nancy stepped over a pile of skirts, jeans, and T-shirts and walked over to locker #9. She remembered that she was using locker

#9 today because the number 9 was the same as the month of September. She opened her locker; her jeans and purple top were hanging neatly on hooks, and her backpack and shoes were lined up at the bottom. She was glad her things weren't all over the floor, like some of the other girls'.

Nancy started to change, then noticed that Nadine was changing a couple of lockers over. Nancy gave her a small wave. "Are you still mad at Antonio for what he did at lunch?" she called out.

Nadine nodded, her eyes blazing. "He almost ruined my Lula Rappaport hoodie! I'll never, ever forgive him!" she said dramatically. Nadine wanted to be an actress when she grew up, so she was always saying things in a theatrical way.

As if on cue, a girl with long, curly red hair walked up to Nadine and tapped her on the shoulder. Nancy recognized her. It was Violet Keeler, a new girl in their class.

"Hey, Nadine? I heard through the grapevine that you have the new Lula Rappaport hoodie," Violet said eagerly. "I don't know if you know this, but I'm the world's biggest Lula fan. In fact, check out this T-shirt. I made it myself."

Violet unzipped her sweatshirt to reveal a white T-shirt. The words LULA ROCKS had been stenciled across the front of it, in pink.

"That's a cool T-shirt," Nancy said.

"Definitely," Nadine agreed. She sat down on a bench and pulled on a pair of yellow polka-dot socks.

Violet tapped Nadine on the shoulder again. "Hey, Nadine? I was wondering. Could I *buy* your Lula hoodie from you? I've looked for it everywhere, but I can't find it. I'll give you my life's savings for it. I have twenty-one dollars and fifty-eight cents. No, twenty-one fifty-nine. *Plus* I have a twenty-five-dollar savings bond that my grandparents gave me. You can cash it in for twenty-five dollars in like five years."

Nadine shrugged apologetically. "Thanks, but I can't sell my hoodie. It was a present from my aunt Chloe, and it's, like, my favorite piece of clothing that I own."

Violet looked disappointed. She thought for a moment. "Then could I just kind of borrow it? For my birthday party, which is going to have a really, really awesome Lula theme? It's in three weeks, and if you let me borrow it, I would totally invite you and make you the guest of honor and everything."

Nadine shook her head. "No, I don't think so." She added, "But I check out clothes websites a lot. I'll let you know if I see the Lula hoodie somewhere."

Violet frowned. "Oh . . . okay. I guess," she mumbled. She sounded disappointed.

Nancy watched as Violet took off. She hadn't known that Violet was such a big Lula Rappaport fan!

"Let's go to my house," Nancy suggested.

"No, let's go to *my* house," Bess said. "My mom baked toffee brownies yesterday. Yum!"

"No, let's go to *my* house," George said. "I want to show you guys this cool new computer game I got. It's called Revenge of the Beastly Bunnies!"

The three of them were standing in front of the school, trying to decide whose house to go to. The air was crisp, and the leaves were just starting to turn gold and red. Nearby, some kids were getting on the bus. Some kids were being picked up by their parents or their sitters. And some kids, like them, were getting ready to walk home by themselves. Nancy was allowed to walk to and from school without grown-ups, since it was less than five blocks from her house.

"Maybe we should flip a coin," Bess suggested. "Except we would need a three-sided coin to decide between our three houses!" She giggled.

Just then, Nadine came rushing up to them.

Her face was flushed, and she looked upset.

"Nadine, what's the matter?" Nancy asked her.

"I have the most awful, horrible news in the world!" Nadine burst out. "My Lula Rappaport hoodie is missing!"

CHAPTER THREE

Too Many Detectives

"What? Are you sure?" George asked Nadine.

"Yes, I'm sure! Some evil thief stole my hoodie. He's probably selling it on the Internet right this minute!" Nadine cried out. "Or maybe it's a *she*. Or maybe it's a he *and* a she," she added.

Nancy thought for a moment. "When was the last time you saw your hoodie, Nadine?"

Nadine considered this. "I saw it in my backpack right before gym class. I remember, because I had to dump everything out to find my gym shorts."

"And when did you notice it was missing?" Nancy asked.

"About five minutes ago. I was at my cubby

getting ready to go home. I wanted to wear my hoodie, so I looked for it in my backpack . . . and it wasn't there!" Nadine's eyes shimmered with tears.

"Are you totally and absolutely positive that you didn't take it out of your backpack or something?" Bess asked her.

"Totally, absolutely, one-hundred-percent positive," Nadine replied. "That means the thief must have stolen it during gym class!"

A bunch of kids raced past them to make the bus. Nancy wondered if any of them—if *any* of her classmates—could have taken Nadine's hoodie. Taking other people's stuff was wrong and mean. On the other hand, maybe Nadine had simply left her hoodie somewhere, and she had forgotten?

"I have an idea. I'll hire the three of you to find my hoodie!" Nadine said suddenly. "How long do you think it will take? Do you charge a lot of money?"

Nancy, George, and Bess were members of a

detective club called the Clue Crew. They had solved lots of mysteries—everything from finding a missing snowman to catching a chicknapper. They were really good at searching for clues and interviewing suspects.

Nancy glanced at George and Bess, who both nodded yes. Nancy turned to Nadine. "We'll accept your case. And we don't charge any money," she said. "I'm not sure how long it will take, though. It depends on how complicated the case is."

"Well, you have to find it soon, because I'm not going to sleep until you do," Nadine insisted.

"If you want to find your hoodie fast, Nadine, then you need to hire *real* detectives," someone said.

Nancy, George, Bess, and Nadine all looked around to see who had spoken. Deirdre was standing behind them on the sidewalk, along with Madison and Kendra.

"Real detectives? What are you talking about?" Nadine asked Deirdre curiously.

"I'm taking about me, Madison, and Kendra. We're the Klue Krew, and you should hire us instead of these inexperienced amateurs," Deirdre said, pointing to Nancy, George, and Bess.

Bess frowned. "What do you mean you're the Clue Crew? *We're* the Clue Crew! Is this a joke, or what?"

"We're the Klue Krew. With K's. As in K-L-U-E K-R-E-W," Deirdre said smugly. "I'm the President and CEO. CEO stands for 'chief executive officer,' in case you didn't know. Here, check out our flier. Kendra?"

Kendra started. "Huh? What, Deirdre?"

"The *fliers*," Deirdre whispered.

"Oh, right." Kendra reached into her backpack and pulled out a pile of bright orange fliers. She passed one each to Nadine, Nancy, George, and Bess.

Nancy scanned her flier. It had a drawing of three girls in trench coats and sunglasses, carrying flashlights and magnifying glasses. It said:

IS YOUR TREE HOUSE HAUNTED?

IS YOUR FAVORITE KITTY MISSING?

ARE YOU GETTING SPOOKY CRANK CALLS?

WELL, DON'T WORRY!

WE'RE THE KLUE KREW, AND WE CAN FIND ANYTHING

AND SOLVE ANY MYSTERY!

WE'RE EXPERIENCED AND RELIABLE.

CONFIDENTIALITY GUARANTEED.

TO GET STARTED, CALL OR E-MAIL DEIRDRE,

THE PRESIDENT AND CEO.

DON'T RELY ON AMATEURS.

COME TO US
FOR ALL YOUR MYSTERY-SOLVING NEEDS!

At the bottom were Deirdre's phone number and e-mail address.

What a bunch of copycats! Nancy thought.

"You're 'experienced'? What mysteries have you solved?" George asked Deirdre, Madison, and Kendra.

"Well, actually—" Madison began.

"We've solved, uh, dozens of mysteries," Deirdre interrupted. "Dozens and dozens, in fact."

Nadine crossed her arms over her chest. "What am I going to do? I don't know if I should hire the Clue Crew with C's or the Klue Krew with K's," she said, confused.

Deirdre's face lit up. "I know! You should hire *both* of us," she said excitedly.

Kendra nodded. "Yeah! We can have a contest."

"Whoever solves the mystery first will become the number-one detective club at River Heights Elementary School!" Madison added.

"We accept!" Bess blurted out. She hesitated. "That is . . . if it's okay with you guys," she said to Nancy and George.

"Game on!" George said. "What do you say, Nancy?"

Nancy grinned. "I'm in."

"Great!" Nadine said eagerly. "With *six* detectives looking for my hoodie instead of three, it'll turn up twice as fast!"

"Okay. We have fifteen minutes until school begins. Let's get started," Nancy said.

It was Wednesday morning. Nancy, George, and Bess were in the girls' locker room. They had come to school extra early so they could look for clues that would lead to the missing hoodie.

On the way to the girls' locker room, they had stopped by the lost-and-found box in the principal's office, just in case the hoodie might be there. But the only things in the box were a baseball cap, a comic book, and a silver hair scrunchie.

Nancy glanced around. It was weird being the only ones in the girls' locker room, which was usually so crowded and noisy—and messy, too. This morning, the locker room was totally quiet. And it seemed to be totally uncluttered, except for a lone white sneaker and a water bottle lying on the floor.

"Which locker did Nadine use yesterday?" George spoke up. There were no preassigned lockers in gym class; each girl used whatever locker was available.

"It must have been number seven, because Nadine's locker was two lockers to the left of mine, and I used number nine," Nancy said after a moment. "I remember that mine was number nine because nine is the same as the month of September."

"You have an awesome memory," Bess complimented her.

Nancy grinned. "Thanks!"

The three girls walked over to locker #7 and opened it. It was empty.

Nancy went over it again, making sure to check every nook and cranny. It was definitely empty. "Hmm," she said, disappointed. "No clues here."

George started opening other lockers. None of them had locks, which made it easy to search them. Nancy and Bess did the same.

"They're all empty," Bess said after a moment. "Except this one—*ew!* There's a pair of stinky socks in here."

"And this one has a stinky pair of gym shorts," George piped up.

The girls kept opening and closing lockers. Nancy glanced at the clock on the wall. School started in five minutes. Time was running out.

Nancy got to locker #24. She was about to open it when she noticed something shiny on the floor in front of it.

She bent down to take a closer look. It was a silver sequin.

Could it be a silver sequin from Nadine's hoodie? she wondered excitedly as she picked it up.

She opened locker #24 to see if there might

be another clue. On the bottom of the locker was something that looked like a crumpled-up candy wrapper. Nancy reached for it and smoothed it out. She was right. It was a Krunchilicious candy wrapper.

"Hey, guys? Who used locker number twenty-four yesterday?" Nancy asked George and Bess.

George glanced up from locker #16. "I don't remember. Do you, Bess?"

Bess was checking out locker #29. "Nope. Why, Nancy?"

"Because I found these two clues," Nancy began. "A silver sequin and a Krunchilicious candy wrapper. I think that—"

Suddenly, there was a noise. It sounded like footsteps.

Nancy put her fingers to her lips. "Shhhh," she

whispered. George and Bess nodded nervously.

The three girls waited and listened. There were more footsteps.

Then Nancy saw something—or rather, *some-one*—peering out from behind a row of lockers.

Nancy's heart began pounding. She, George, and Bess weren't alone anymore.

Could it be the thief, returning to the scene of the crime?

chaPTER FOUR

Breaking News

Nancy wasn't sure what to do. Should she, George, and Bess try to hide . . . or run for it . . . or face the thief . . . or what? She had to make a split-second decision.

We should face the thief—or whoever it is, she thought.

Nancy cupped her hands over her mouth. "Come out! We know you're there!" she called loudly.

In response, the person jumped out from behind the row of lockers. Then a second person jumped out. Then a third.

All three people were dressed in matching trench coats and dark glasses. Nancy stared and stared. They looked like the pictures on the Klue Krew's flier. . . .

"Deirdre?" she said after a moment. "Madison? Kendra?"

Deirdre adjusted her dark glasses. "We're undercover, so please don't use our real names!" she said conspiratorially. "What are you three doing in here, anyway?"

"Uh, we're working on our case," George said.

"You mean you're working on *our* case," Deirdre corrected her. "Soooo. I bet you haven't found anything, have you?"

"Actually, Nancy just found—" Bess began, then clamped her hand over her mouth. "I mean . . . Nancy didn't find anything. Anything at all."

Deirdre frowned. "Hmm. You're hiding something, aren't you? Well, not for long!" She turned to Madison and Kendra. "Come on, Agent Double Oh One and Agent Double Oh Two. We've got exactly three minutes and twelve seconds to do a complete search of the premises. Go, go, *go!* You have your orders!"

"Yes, Chief!" Madison and Kendra said in unison.

Madison and Kendra took a couple of flashlights and magnifying glasses out of their coat pockets and started checking out all the lockers. Nancy tried to stifle a laugh. The Klue Krew seemed to be taking their jobs a little too seriously!

❀ ❀ ❀

"Let's go over what we have so far," Nancy said.

It was after school on Wednesday. Nancy, George, and Bess were hanging out in Nancy's room, discussing the case. Nancy's puppy, Chocolate Chip, was curled up on the floor, snoring and thumping her tail.

Nancy and Bess were sitting cross-legged on the bed, which had a pretty lavender-and-white bedspread that matched the rest of Nancy's room. Nancy had her special purple detective notebook on her lap. It was the notebook she used to keep track of all the Clue Crew cases, in purple pencil.

George was sitting in front of Nancy's computer. She liked to keep track of all the Clue Crew cases on the computer. "Okay. I'm going to open a new file, and I'm going to call it 'The Case of the Missing Hoodie,'" she announced.

"Good idea," Nancy said. She flipped through the notebook and started scribbling some notes onto a fresh page. "So. We have two clues: the silver sequin and the Krunchilicious candy wrapper."

Nancy reached into her backpack and pulled out a small plastic bag. Inside the bag were the sequin and the candy wrapper. She always carried small plastic bags for storing clues, "in case of a case."

She handed the bag to George, who put it inside Nancy's desk drawer. The drawer was full of bags containing clues from all their cases, old and new. Nancy sometimes thought of the drawer as a clue museum!

George turned back to the computer. "Okay, so what about suspects?"

"I think Antonio is the thief," Bess blurted out. "He pretended to trip and spill chili all over Nadine's hoodie yesterday, remember? Maybe he pretended to steal it, too. He loves to pull evil pranks like that."

Nancy thought about this. "Yeah, except . . . Nadine said she saw her hoodie in her backpack at the beginning of gym class. And right after gym class, she noticed it was missing. Which means that the thief probably stole the hoodie in the girls' locker room. How would Antonio get into the girls' locker room?"

Bess frowned. "Oh. Hmm. Maybe Antonio was working with a partner? A girl partner?" she suggested.

"He should definitely be on the suspect list, even though he's a boy," George agreed, typing. "Who else?"

"Well, there's that new girl, Violet Keeler," Nancy said. "I heard her talking to Nadine in the locker room yesterday. She's a big, huge Lula Rappaport fan. She was practically begging Nadine to sell her the hoodie, or at least let her borrow it for her birthday party. Nadine said no. Violet seemed kind of upset."

"Maybe Violet is Antonio's partner, then," Bess mused.

"We should interview both of them tomorrow," George suggested.

"Good idea," Nancy said. "And don't forget—we also have the results of our Krunchilicious poll."

Nancy, George, and Bess had conducted a poll at lunchtime: Krunchilicious versus Choco Mania. Nancy had a theory that whoever had used locker #24 yesterday might be the hoodie thief, because the silver sequin was in front of locker #24. So it was important to know who liked Krunchilicious candy bars and who didn't, since they had found the Krunchilicious candy wrapper in locker #24.

The results had been interesting. Most of the kids they had polled preferred Choco-Mania. The only Krunchilicious fans were Deirdre, Madison, Kendra, Violet, and Antonio.

There was a knock on Nancy's door. "Come in!" the girls called out in unison.

Hannah Gruen walked in, carrying a tray. Hannah was the Drews' housekeeper. She had been with Nancy and her father, Carson Drew, since Nancy's mother had died five years ago. But Hannah was much more than a housekeeper. She brushed Nancy's hair every night, gave great hugs, and made the world's yummiest vegetable lasagna.

"Hi, Hannah!" Nancy said, waving and smiling. "What did you bring us?"

Hannah chuckled as she set the tray down on the bed. "Well, I figured you girls were working hard on your new mystery. So I brought you some power snacks to help you brainstorm. Banana bread and hot apple cider. What do you think?"

"We think that's awesome!" Bess said excitedly. "Thanks, Hannah!"

"You're welcome, detectives!"

After Hannah left, the girls dug into the snacks. They were delicious. "So where were we?" Nancy started to say, just as a little bell *ding*ed on her computer.

George glanced at the screen. "You have an instant message from Nadine," she told Nancy. "She says we need to see Deirdre's website ASAP."

"Huh? Why?" Bess said.

"I'll check it out," George said as she typed in

the address for Dishing with Deirdre. Deirdre used her website to post articles, gossip, photos, and whatever else she felt like posting, including her opinions on just about everything. Nancy and Bess got up from the bed and stood behind George as the homepage appeared.

All three girls gasped when they saw the enormous headline blazing across the screen:

**THE INTERNATIONALLY FAMOUS
KLUE KREW DETECTIVE CLUB IS CLOSE
TO CRACKING THE HOODIE MYSTERY!**

ChaPTeR FiVe

A Ransom Note

"What is Deirdre talking about?" Bess exclaimed. "How did they find Nadine's hoodie already?"

"Let's keep reading," Nancy suggested.

Under the blazing headline, Deirdre had posted an article. It read:

> The Klue Krew is klose to klosing a major kase! (LOL!)
>
> Yesterday, River Heights Elementary School student Nadine Nardo was the victim of a vicious crime. Her brand-new pink Lula Rappaport hoodie was stolen from the girls' locker room!
>
> "Please find it for me!" a sobbing

Nadine begged "DS," the President and CEO of the Klue Krew. (For security reasons, the Klue Krew will not reveal the identities of its members.)

Nadine also hired Nancy Drew and her "Clue Crew" for the same case. Rumor has it that Nadine felt sorry for them because they didn't have any other cases to work on.

As of 3:32 p.m. today, the Klue Krew has found dozens and dozens of clues. The Klue Krew has also interviewed dozens and dozens of witnesses and suspects. "I think Nadine will have her hoodie back any minute now," said "MF," a Klue Krew agent.

"We're really close to solving the mystery," said "KJ," another Klue Krew agent. "On the other hand, Nancy Drew and her Clue Crew are totally clueless!"

❀ ❀ ❀

"This article is a pack of lies!" Bess said angrily.

"It's just Deirdre being Deirdre," George reassured her. "We should ignore it."

"Definitely," Nancy agreed.

"But everyone will read it and think they're a better detective club than our Clue Crew!" Bess pointed out. "Deirdre can't get away with this! Here, George, scoot over."

She gave George a little push and sat down in her place in front of Nancy's computer. She began typing, her fingers flying across the keyboard.

"What are you doing, Bess?" Nancy asked her curiously.

"You'll see," Bess replied mysteriously.

After a second, the IM window popped up on the screen. Nancy realized that Bess was IMing Deirdre.

Bess typed: YR WEBSITE IS FULL OF LIES!!!!!

Deirdre typed: YR JUST JEALOUS B/C KK ROCKS AND CC DOESNT

Bess typed: CC IS WAY AHEAD OF KK

Deirdre typed: YOU GUYS HAVENT FOUND ANYTHING

Bess typed: YES WE HAVE!!!!!!!!

Deirdre typed: UR LYING

Bess typed: WE FOUND KRUN

"*BESS!*" Nancy and George yelled at the same time.

Bess accidentally hit ENTER. "Huh? What?"

"You have to stop typing right this second!" Nancy told her. "Deirdre is just trying to trick you into telling her top-secret information."

Bess blushed. "Oh. I'm sorry! I almost typed 'Krunchilicious.'"

"Sign off, sign off," George urged Bess.

Bess typed: GOTTA GO! Then she signed off. "Sorry, guys," she apologized to Nancy and George. "That was close! I mean, that was 'klose' with a *K*!"

"What are you making, Violet?" Nancy asked her in a friendly voice.

It was Thursday morning. Nancy and her classmates were in art class, creating collages out of magazine clippings and brightly colored tissue paper.

Violet was at the same table as Nancy, George, and Bess. Nancy had decided to take the opportunity to question Violet, since she was a suspect. Deirdre, Madison, and Kendra were sitting all the way across the room. They didn't seem to be paying any attention to Nancy and her Clue Crew.

Violet held up her collage with a proud smile. The collage had lots of photos of Lula Rappaport. There was Lula on the set of one of her movies. There was Lula air-kissing her fans. There was Lula inline skating with her six toy poodles. There was Lula getting a manicure at a fancy-looking spa.

"I'm going to call this 'The Many Faces of Lula,'" Violet said. "I really hope I get an A on it."

"I'm sure you will!" Nancy said. "By the way, speaking of Lula . . . you know about Nadine's missing hoodie, right?"

Violet's brown eyes widened. "I know what you're going to say!" she burst out before Nancy could say another word. "You're going to say that *I'm* the one who stole it, aren't you? Of course you would say that, since I'm, like, the biggest Lula Rappaport fan in the entire universe. But there's no way I would ever, ever steal someone else's Lula hoodie. Stealing is wrong!"

Nancy, George, and Bess exchanged glances. "I wasn't going to say you stole it," Nancy told Violet. "I was just going to ask you if you knew anything about it. Anything at all. It would really help our case."

"I don't know anything," Violet said huffily. "Now, if you'll excuse me, I have to get more glitter glue." She turned and marched over to the art supply closet.

"I guess she's not talking," Nancy said to her friends.

"I guess not. But there's our other suspect, right over there." George nodded at Antonio, who was working on a collage two tables over.

"Hmm. I'm going to go talk to him," Nancy said. "You guys stay here in case Violet changes her mind and decides to say something."

"Okey-dokey," Bess said.

Nancy went over to Antonio's table and peered at the collage he was working on. It had lots of photos of slimy-looking reptiles, like crocodiles and lizards and snakes. "That's um, really cool," she complimented him.

Antonio's face lit up. "Yeah? You like reptiles?"

"Um, definitely!" Nancy fibbed. She decided to change the subject, fast. "So. Did you hear about Nadine's hoodie?"

"You mean that pink thing? What, did it get hit with a *real* chili bomb?" Antonio cracked up.

Nancy frowned. "No. It's missing. It might have been stolen. You knew that, right?"

"Stolen? Who would steal that ugly old thing?" Antonio said. He picked up a glue stick and started smearing it across the back of a photo. He got glue all over the table.

"You mean you really didn't know?" Nancy asked him.

"Huh? Why would I know? And why would I care?" Antonio said.

All of a sudden, Antonio picked up photo he was working on and lunged at Nancy's face with it. She gave a little gasp and jumped back. She didn't want to get a photo of an alligator glued to her nose!

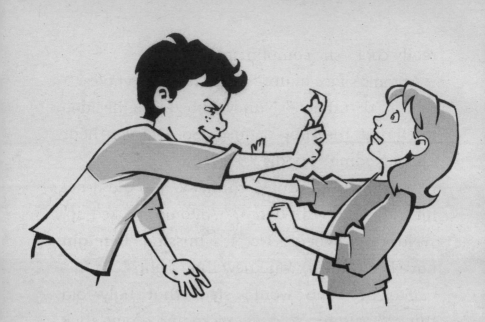

"Ha-ha," Antonio crowed.

Nancy glared at him. Would he *ever* stop pulling pranks?

At lunch, Nancy filled George and Bess in on her conversation with Antonio.

"He *said* he didn't know about the hoodie," Nancy explained as she took a bite of her grilled cheese sandwich.

"Do you think he was lying?" George asked her.

Nancy shrugged. "I'm not sure. I couldn't tell. He's definitely evil, though. Evil enough to steal Nadine's hoodie."

"Well, we didn't get anything else out of Violet, either," Bess said. She stirred her chocolate milk with a straw. "I think she's hiding something, though. She was acting kind of weird."

"Weird? What do you mean, weird?" Nancy asked her.

But before Bess could answer, Nadine came rushing up to their table. "Guess what!" she cried out. She sounded upset.

"What?" Nancy, George, and Bess said in unison.

Nadine waved a folded-up piece of paper in the air. "I just got a ransom note from the hoodie-napper!" she announced.

ChaPTER Six

Kopy Kats

"A ransom note?" Nancy said, alarmed. That sounded pretty serious. "What does it say?"

"Here." Nadine quickly unfolded the sheet of paper.

Nancy, George, and Bess bent their heads together to read it. The ransom note was written in pencil on a piece of wide-ruled notebook paper. It said:

IF YOU WANT YOU'RE HOODY
BACK, YOU'LL HAVE TO PAY!
WAIT FOR MORE INSTRUCSHIONS.

Nancy read the ransom note again. She noticed the handwriting was kind of messy, with big, loopy letters.

She also noticed that it had some spelling mistakes in it. YOU'RE should have been YOUR. HOODY should have been HOODIE. And INSTRUCSHIONS should have been INSTRUC-TIONS.

Nancy glanced up after a moment. "Where did you find this, Nadine?"

"I found it in my cubby, just now," Nadine replied. She wrung her hands together. "Do you think my hoodie is in danger? Do you think I'll have to pay the person a lot of money to get it back? Like millions and millions of dollars?"

"It said we're supposed to wait for instructions," George pointed out. "I wonder if the hoodie-napper is going to leave another note in your cubby."

"Maybe we should install secret video cameras on your cubby, to catch the person leaving the next note," Bess suggested. "Hmm.

I guess that might be kind of hard, though."

"Can we keep this note?" Nancy asked Nadine.

"I have to show it to the Klue Krew with K's first. They haven't seen it yet. You can have it back after that," Nadine promised her.

"No problem," Nancy agreed.

Nadine folded up the note and walked over to Deirdre's table, across the aisle. Nancy watched as Deirdre, Madison, and Kendra checked out the note.

Deirdre got a purple notebook out of her backpack and started scribbling furiously in it.

It looked just like Nancy's purple detective note-book. She was even using a purple pencil like Nancy's.

Talk about a copycat! Nancy thought, amused.

And then she frowned. *Is the Klue Krew close to solving the case?* she wondered. *Or are they as clueless as they say we are?*

"I think we should get an extra-extra-large pizza with extra-extra cheese and extra-extra pepperoni," Bess suggested.

"Sounds good to me," Carson Drew said, closing his menu. "Okay with you girls?"

"Yum!" Nancy said.

"Extra-extra yum!" George agreed.

It was Thursday night. Nancy's father had taken Nancy, George, and Bess to Pizza Paradise for dinner as a special treat. It was early, and the downtown pizza parlor was just starting to get crowded.

The waitress came by to take their orders. After she left, Mr. Drew said, "So, I guess the

Clue Crew has been busy solving another mystery?"

"We haven't solved it yet, Daddy," Nancy said. "We found some important clues, though."

"And we have two suspects!" George piped up.

"*And* we have competition," Bess added, making a face. "Deirdre Shannon formed a detective club called the Klue Krew. With K's. They're trying to solve the mystery, too."

"Really? Who's winning so far? The Clue Crew with C's or the Klue Krew with K's?" Mr. Drew asked.

"We don't know, Daddy," Nancy replied.

Mr. Drew put his arm around Nancy. "Well, Pumpkin Pie, I'm rooting for the three of you!"

The waitress brought them a pitcher of lemonade and four glasses. While Mr. Drew poured the lemonades, Nancy filled him in on the case. She told him about the silver sequin and the Krunchilicious wrapper. She told him about the Krunchilicious versus Choco-Mania poll. She told him about Violet and Antonio being their top suspects. And she told him about the ransom note with the spelling mistakes.

"We still need to figure out who used locker number twenty-four on Tuesday," Nancy finished. "Plus we need to figure out who wrote the ransom note. They could be the same person—or not."

Mr. Drew looked thoughtful. "You said that the hoodie was stolen from the girls' locker room, right? How could the thief be a boy, then?"

"Maybe Antonio was working with a girl, like Violet or someone else," George replied. "Or maybe Antonio snuck into the girls' locker room."

"Ewwwww!" Bess exclaimed.

At the mention of Antonio's name, Nancy suddenly remembered something. She remembered that his family owned a restaurant across the street from Pizza Paradise. She craned her head to peer out the window. She saw the sign for Chez Fano. Antonio had told her once that Fano was short for his last name, Elefano.

At that moment, she saw Antonio walking briskly down the sidewalk, heading for Chez

Fano. At one point, he tripped on something, and he almost fell. His backpack slipped off his shoulders and fell to the ground. He muttered something to himself, picked up his backpack, and hurried into the restaurant.

Nancy spun around in her seat. Her eyes were sparkling.

"What is it, Pumpkin Pie?" her father asked her.

"I think Antonio wrote the ransom note!" she announced.

ChAPTER SEVEN

Mystery Solved?

"Why do you think Antonio wrote the ransom note?" George asked Nancy.

"*Ew!* That means he definitely snuck into the girls' locker room!" Bess said, wrinkling her nose.

"I don't know about that," Nancy said quickly. "But remember? On Tuesday, in the cafeteria, Antonio pretended to trip and spill his chili all over Nadine's hoodie. His backpack fell on the floor, and his stuff fell out—like his pencils and math homework and spelling test. I saw his spelling test. It had lots and lots of mistakes on it."

George nodded. "And we know whoever wrote the ransom note was a bad speller!"

"Does his handwriting match the handwriting on the ransom note?" Mr. Drew piped up.

Nancy, George, and Bess stared at each other.

"I'm not sure," Nancy said after a moment. "That's a smart question, though, Daddy. We should check out Antonio's handwriting and see if it matches the handwriting on the note!"

"We should make you an honorary Clue Crew member, Mr. Drew," George said.

Mr. Drew chuckled. "It sounds like there are already too many detectives on this case!"

After dinner, Nancy, George, Bess, and Mr. Drew went across the street to Chez Fano. Nancy had been watching the front entrance the whole time they were eating their pizzas. As far as she could tell, Antonio was still there.

Chez Fano was one of the fanciest restaurants in River Heights. It was in an elegant-looking brick building with a red door. The windows had pretty lace curtains and window boxes full of orange and yellow chrysanthemums.

Inside, there was a crowded waiting area with plush velvet chairs and potted palm trees. A man in a black tuxedo was standing in the doorway to the dining room. Nancy recognized him from a previous trip to Chez Fano. He was the maitre d', in charge of seating customers.

"Dinner for four?" he asked Mr. Drew.

"Actually—" Mr. Drew began.

"Actually, we're here to see Antonio," Nancy interrupted. "Is he here?"

"Little Tony? I'll get him," the maitre d' offered.

Little Tony? Nancy, George, and Bess looked at each other and giggled.

The maitre d' disappeared through the doorway. Nancy could hear soft classical music, clinking glasses, conversation, and laughter coming from the dining room. Delicious spicy smells wafted through the air. As they waited, customers left and more customers came in. Chez Fano was a busy place!

After a moment, Antonio appeared. He

frowned in confusion when he saw Nancy, George, and Bess.

"Uh, hi," Antonio said. Nancy could tell that he was trying hard to be polite, since her father was there. "Uh, what do you want? That is . . . I mean . . . can I help you with something?"

Nancy reached into her backpack and found a pen and a blank piece of paper. "Can you write down the phone number for your family's restaurant, Antonio?" she asked in a friendly voice. "It's George's mom's birthday this weekend, and we want to make a reservation for dinner."

George made a face. "What? My mom's birthday is—"

"I mean, it's George's *dad's* birthday," Nancy cut in. She winked at George to let her know that she was making up a story so she could get a sample of Antonio's handwriting. "So, Antonio . . . could you write down the phone number? And the name of the restaurant, too," she added.

Antonio took the pen and paper from Nancy. He started scribbling.

Nancy leaned over and watched as Antonio wrote the information down. She saw that his handwriting was messy and big and loopy—just like on the ransom note!

"You *did* write the ransom note!" Nancy burst out. "Okay, Antonio—where's Nadine's hoodie?"

Antonio's head shot up. "Huh? What are you talking about?"

Nancy pulled the ransom note out of her backpack. She placed it next to the piece of paper Antonio had been scribbling on. The handwriting was identical!

"You are *so* busted," Bess told Antonio.

Antonio's face turned red. "Okay. So I wrote the ransom note. Big deal. It was just a joke!" he mumbled. "But I didn't steal the hoodie. I swear! You can come to my house right now and search through all my stuff if you want!"

Nancy was about to ask him another question. But she was distracted by something. One of the potted palm trees in the waiting area was . . . *moving.* Or rather, the palm fronds were moving this way and that, as though there was a breeze. It didn't make sense, since they were inside.

Nancy walked over to the palm tree and peered behind it. Someone was hiding there.

Actually, it was *three* someones: Deirdre, Madison, and Kendra—the Klue Krew!

When Deirdre saw Nancy, she stepped out from behind the palm tree. She tucked her hair behind her ear and smiled.

"Oh! Hi, Nancy! What are you doing here?" she asked casually.

"What are *you* doing here?" Nancy asked her curiously.

"We're, uh . . . we're, uh . . . checking out the menu," Deirdre said. "But we have to run. Bye!"

"Bye!" Madison and Kendra said in unison.

Then, without another word, the three girls ran out the door. Nancy frowned. What was going on? Had the Klue Krew followed the Clue Crew to Chez Fano and eavesdropped on their conversation with Antonio?

Just then, Nancy noticed a purple object on the floor. It was her purple detective notebook. Had she dropped it? When? Did anyone else see it? She picked it up and flipped through the pages.

Nancy saw right away that it *wasn't* her notebook. On one of the pages was a drawing of Nadine's hoodie. There was another drawing of three girls with a big X through it. Nancy studied the three girls' faces. They kind of looked like her, George, and Bess!

Then Nancy's eyes fell on a long, hand-written entry. It said:

Day One. Hoodie disappears! Good timing.

Day Two. Discovered CC in girls' locker room. Agent B said Agent N found something. We think it was a pair of stinky socks that belonged to the thief. Must find out who wears Sporty Girl brand socks. Later, Agent B IMs that they found "Krun." What is "Krun"? What does it mean?

Day Three. We now think stinky socks were a red herring. A red herring is a false clue that's meant to throw us off the scent and confuse us. Who planted the stinky socks, and why? Was it CC? Also, we are adding the gym teacher to the suspect list because Agent 001 says she heard him humming a Lula song under his breath. So the gym teacher is a Lula fan. Sounds pretty guilty!

Nancy closed the notebook. She didn't want to read any more. It was an invasion of Deirdre's privacy. In fact, she would have to get the notebook back to Deirdre right away.

Then Nancy smiled. From what little she *had* read, it seemed that the Klue Krew was pretty *klue*less! There was no way they were going to win the contest.

Then Nancy's smile faded. The Clue Crew wasn't much further along than the Klue Krew. If they didn't find more clues soon, they wouldn't win the contest either!

"Did you find my hoodie?" Nadine asked. "Please, please, please tell me you did!"

It was Friday morning, just before school. Nancy, George, Bess, and Nadine were in the hallway, talking. Kids swarmed around them, talking and laughing as they headed for their cubbies.

Nancy shook her head. "No. But we did find who wrote the—"

"*We* found your hoodie, Nadine!"

The girls turned to see who had spoken. It was Deirdre. Madison and Kendra were standing behind her.

Nancy couldn't believe it. Had the Klue Krew really solved the mystery before the Clue Crew?

CHAPTER EIGHT

Too Many Hoodies

Deirdre had a smug-looking grin on her face. Nancy noticed that Madison and Kendra didn't look quite as smug. In fact, they were both staring down at the ground, as though they didn't want to meet Nadine's eyes.

What was going on?

Nadine rushed up to Deirdre. "You found my hoodie? Where? How? When? Who?" she said excitedly.

"The 'who' is easy. It was Antonio Elefano!" Deirdre announced. "We figured out last night that Antonio wrote the ransom note. From there, it was easy to figure out that he was the hoodie thief."

Nancy gasped. Deirdre and her Klue Krew were being copycats again! They had eavesdropped on the Clue Crew last night at Chez Fano. Antonio had confessed to writing the ransom note. From that, the Klue Krew had obviously concluded that Antonio was the thief.

"Do you have any proof against Antonio?" Nancy asked Deirdre.

"We have something better than proof. We have this!" Deirdre said.

She reached into her backpack and pulled out something pink and silver.

It was Nadine's hoodie!

"Oh my gosh!" Nadine cried out. She grabbed the hoodie from Deirdre and hugged it to her chest. She started jumping up and down. "Thank you, thank you, thank you! I never thought I'd see this again. I never thought—*Heyyyy!*"

"What is it?" George asked Nadine.

Nadine was staring at the label on the back of the hoodie. "This . . . is *not* . . . my hoodie," she said slowly.

"Of *course* it's your hoodie!" Deirdre said quickly. "Now, as for payment. We're not going to charge you, Nadine, since it's your first case with us. But I think it's fair to say that the Klue Krew with K's beat the Clue Crew with C's, so we definitely won the contest. You might want to make us some sort of certificate saying so. You

know, like 'I, Nadine Nardo, hereby congratu-
late the Klue Krew with K's for defeating the
Clue Crew with C's and becoming the number-one
detective club in all of River Heights Elementary
School.'"

Nadine glared at Deirdre. "I'm serious! This is
not my hoodie! Check out the label. This isn't
my size. And besides, I wrote my initials on the
label with a black Magic Marker. This label
doesn't have any initials on it."

Deirdre studied the label. "Maybe you just
thought you wrote your initials," she said
smoothly. "Or maybe the thief—that is, I mean,
Antonio—erased the initials with some sort
of, you know, special Magic Marker–erasing
potion."

"Deirdre!" Madison whispered at her. "Tell
her the truth!"

"Yeah, Deirdre, you should tell her," Kendra
piped up.

"Tell me *what*?" Nadine demanded.

Deirdre sighed. "Okay. So this isn't your

hoodie, Nadine. It's the one my dad ordered for me. It came in the mail yesterday."

"And you were going to *pretend* it was my hoodie so you could be the number-one detective club in school?" Nadine asked her.

"Well! I thought you'd be grateful that we found *a* Lula Rappaport hoodie, even if it wasn't *the* Lula Rappaport hoodie," Deirdre said huffily.

"I want *my* Lula hoodie, not just any Lula hoodie," Nadine replied.

"Fine. The Klue Krew with K's will not give up until this case is solved," Deirdre said firmly.

"Speaking of the case . . . you dropped this last night at Chez Fano," Nancy said. She reached into her backpack and pulled out Deirdre's purple notebook.

Deirdre grabbed the notebook from Nancy. "And speaking of *thieves* . . . you stole this so you could get valuable information from us, Nancy Drew!" she said accusingly.

"You *dropped* it," Nancy insisted.

"You *stole* it!" Deirdre said.

Just then, the school bell rang. Deirdre shot Nancy a nasty look and strode off. *Saved by the bell,* Nancy thought.

Saturday morning was gray and cloudy, as though it might start raining at any moment. As Nancy, George, and Bess walked together to Violet's house, they stepped in piles of autumn leaves with their rain boots, making crunchy sounds.

"Maybe we'll get more information out of Violet this time," Nancy said hopefully.

"She's still our top suspect, and so is Antonio, even though he *says* he didn't steal Nadine's hoodie," Bess agreed.

George started tapping the sidewalk with her umbrella. "Guys? I thought of another suspect. Actually, *three* suspects."

"Who?" Nancy asked her curiously.

"The Klue Krew with K's," George replied.

Bess frowned at her cousin. "Huh? How could

Deirdre, Madison, and Kendra *be* the thieves? They're trying to *find* the thief."

"I know," George said. "But don't you think the timing is kind of funny? Remember Tuesday, at the end of the day? Nadine told us that her hoodie was missing. A few minutes later, Deirdre, Madison, and Kendra showed up with their Klue Krew fliers and offered to solve the case. What if they pretended to steal the hoodie so they could pretend to solve the case?"

"Deirdre is pretty sneaky. She would do something like that," Bess said thoughtfully.

"Yeah, she is sneaky," Nancy said thoughtfully. "Maybe we should add them to the suspect list after all."

The girls soon reached Violet's house. It was a small green bungalow with purple shutters. Nancy could see a swing set in the backyard.

They went up to the front door and rang the bell. After a moment, a short, red-haired woman answered.

"Can I help you?" she asked in a friendly voice.

"Is Violet home?" Nancy asked her. "We're in her class at school. I'm Nancy, and this is George and Bess."

"Oh, hello!" the woman said. "I'm her mom, Mrs. Keeler. I'm so glad Violet has new friends! We just moved to River Heights a couple of months ago." She peered over her shoulder. "I think Violet's in her room. Why don't you girls come in and wait while I go and get her?"

"Thank you!" Bess said.

Nancy, George, and Bess went inside and stood in the hallway while Mrs. Keeler headed upstairs. Nancy glanced around. There was a neat row of boots and shoes along one wall. There was a coat rack along another.

A fluffy white cat came up to them and circled their ankles, purring. "Hi, kitty," Nancy said.

She bent down to pet it and noticed a backpack next to the row of boots and shoes. It had Lula stickers all over it. *It must be Violet's,* Nancy thought.

Then Nancy noticed something else. There was a sweatshirt peeking out of the backpack. It was pink—the exact same color pink as Nadine's hoodie. Nancy could also make out some sparkly silver sequins on it.

Nancy jumped to her feet. "Violet is the hoodie thief!" she whispered excitedly to George and Bess.

CHAPTER NINE

Two More Lockers

"Violet is the hoodie thief?" George whispered.

"How do you know, Nancy?" Bess piped up.

Nancy pointed to the pink fabric spilling out of Violet's backpack. "That looks exactly like the Lula hoodie."

"Oh my gosh, it does!" Bess agreed.

Nancy knelt down to take a closer look at the hoodie. Just then, she heard an angry voice: "What are you doing in my backpack, Nancy Drew?"

Nancy leaped to her feet. Violet was at the top of the stairs. Mrs. Keeler was not with her. From somewhere in the house, Nancy could hear her talking on the phone.

Violet trotted down the stairs. "I said what are you doing in my backpack?" she demanded.

"I—that is—" Nancy tried to think of what to say.

Bess put her hands on her hips. "We found Nadine's hoodie in your backpack, Violet Keeler!" she exclaimed. "*You're* the hoodie thief. You'd better 'fess up right now!"

Violet's jaw dropped open. Her cheeks turned bright red. "I-I told you before. I-I'm not the hoodie thief!" she stammered.

"If you didn't steal Nadine's hoodie, then how did it get in your backpack?" George asked her.

"It's not Nadine's hoodie!" Violet replied.

"What do you mean, it's not Nadine's hoodie?" Nancy said.

Violet sighed. She reached down and pulled the hoodie out of her backpack.

She held it up for Nancy, George, and Bess to see. It looked exactly like Nadine's hoodie.

"I know what you're thinking," Violet said quickly. "But it's not Nadine's. I made it myself a couple of days ago. I bought a plain hoodie that was the same shade of pink as Nadine's. I bought some silver sequins, fabric glue, and a silver Magic Marker, too. I did the best I could, but it's not exactly, one-hundred-percent the same."

Violet pointed to the silver sequin heart in back. "The original Lula hoodie has fifty silver sequins. Mine has only forty. I ran out of sequins! And I didn't get the heart exactly right. Plus, see the label? The original Lula hoodie says 'Design by Lula' on it. This one says 'Hoodie Central' on it."

Nancy studied Violet's hoodie. She was right. "How do you know so much about the original Lula hoodie, Violet?" she asked curiously.

"I . . . uh . . . well . . ." Violet

dropped her eyes to the ground. "Okay, I'll confess. On Tuesday, I overheard you guys talking about Nadine's hoodie during lunch. I really, really wanted to check it out. So later, during gym class, I kind of snuck back into the girls' locker room. I told the teacher I had to go to the bathroom. Then I went into Nadine's locker and opened her backpack so I could take a super-close look. I even made some sketches of it so I could copy it."

"You did all that?" George said, surprised.

"I know it was wrong," Violet admitted. "Anyway, I guess I wasn't watching the clock, because all of a sudden gym class was over and everyone started running back into the locker room. I didn't know what to do. I kind of panicked and threw Nadine's hoodie onto a pile of clothes on the floor. Everything was such a mess in there, I didn't think Nadine would notice."

"Why did you ask Nadine if you could buy or borrow her hoodie while we were all changing?" Nancy asked her.

"I really meant it. I wanted to buy it or at least

borrow it. I knew that would be even better than having a copycat Lula hoodie," Violet said.

Nancy thought about Violet's words. "Why didn't you tell Nadine about throwing her hoodie on the floor after you found out that her hoodie was missing?" she asked after a moment.

Violet shrugged. "I didn't want her to be mad at me. I guess I should tell her, though, huh?"

"Did you use locker number twenty-four on Tuesday, Violet?" George piped up. "And did you leave a Krunchilicious wrapper in the locker?"

"Yes and yes," Violet replied. "Krunchilicious bars are my favorite things in the world— besides Lula Rappaport hoodies!"

Bess turned to Nancy and George. "Well, that explains the silver sequin and the Krunchilicious wrapper," she said.

Nancy nodded. "Yeah. But it still doesn't explain where Nadine's hoodie is!" She added, "I think we all need to go over to her house right now. Violet, can we use your phone to get permission from our parents?"

❀ ❀ ❀

Fifteen minutes later, Nancy, George, Bess, and Violet were standing on Nadine's front porch. Nancy rang the doorbell, and Nadine's dad let them in. "Nadine, your friends are here!" he called up the stairs.

Nadine came downstairs and joined the girls in the living room. "Hi!" she said excitedly. "What's up? Did you solve the mystery? Why is Violet with you? Is she a new Clue Crew member?"

Nancy glanced at Violet. "Violet has something to tell you."

Nadine glared at Violet. "Did *you* steal my hoodie?" she asked suspiciously.

Violet shook her head. Then she explained what she had done on Tuesday afternoon, during gym class.

"I'm really, really, really super-sorry," she said when she had finished. "I know it's wrong to look at other people's stuff without their permission."

Nadine frowned. "Maybe the thief saw you checking out my hoodie and decided to steal it.

Maybe this is all your fault!" she said accusingly.

"I feel really bad. Maybe I could use my life's savings and buy you a new hoodie?" Violet offered.

Nadine sighed. "It's okay. I guess. At least you confessed and apologized and all that." She turned to Nancy. "I'm starting to feel like I'm never, ever going to see my hoodie again," she added in a gloomy voice.

"I've been thinking," Nancy said. "On Tuesday, you used locker number seven. And I used locker number nine. Do you remember who used the locker between us? Locker number eight? Was it Kendra, maybe?"

Nadine nodded. "It was definitely Kendra."

"What about number six, the locker on the other side of you?" Nancy asked her.

"Hmm . . . it was Madison," Nadine said after a moment.

"Why are you asking her about those two lockers?" Bess asked Nancy.

"I think I just solved the case of the missing hoodie!" Nancy announced.

But before she could say any more, the doorbell rang. A moment later, Nadine's father showed four more girls into the living room.

It was Deirdre, Madison, and Kendra—plus a girl with short blond hair. Nancy recognized her as a fifth-grader from their school. She tried to think of her name. Kathy? Kaitlin?

"Uh, hi, guys," Nadine said, frowning. "What's up?"

"We won the contest!" Deirdre crowed triumphantly. "We solved the case!"

CHAPTER TEN

And the Winner Is . . .

Nadine stared at Deirdre. Then she stared at Nancy. "I'm confused," she said after a moment. "Did the Clue Crew with C's solve the case? Or the Klue Krew with K's?"

"*We* solved the case, dummy," Deirdre said quickly. She pointed to the girl with short blond hair. "Ta-da! This is your hoodie thief. Her name is Kelly Krunfeld!"

"*That's* why you dragged me over here, Deirdre? Because you think I stole somebody's hoodie?" the girl named Kelly Krunfeld burst out. "You said you wanted to interview me for your website. You lied!"

"A detective has to do whatever is necessary

to solve a crime," Deirdre replied simply. "Anyway, Nadine—Kelly here is your thief. The Klue Krew with K's figured this out based on a superimportant clue we found—the letters K-R-U-N."

Nancy, George, and Bess exchanged a glance. Then they burst out laughing.

"Why are you laughing?" Madison asked them.

"Yeah, what's so funny?" Kendra piped up.

"You guys got that K-R-U-N clue from us," Bess explained. "I IMed it to Deirdre by mistake. But it's not part of your name, Kelly. It's part of the word Krunchilicious. We found a Krunchilicious candy wrapper in one of the lockers in the girls' locker room. It's one of our clues."

"What?" Madison and Kendra said at the same time. They both stared at Deirdre.

Deirdre shrugged. "Big deal. So I made a mistake."

"You sure did! I'm going home," Kelly said huffily.

After Kelly was gone, Nadine turned to Nancy.

"I guess the Klue Krew with K's didn't solve the case after all. What about the Clue Crew with C's?"

"I think I know what happened," Nancy said. "Hey, Kendra? Do you use a gym bag for gym? Or do you keep your gym clothes in your backpack?"

"I use a gym bag," Kendra said. "Why are you asking me that?"

"Have you checked it lately? Was there anything in there that wasn't yours?" Nancy went on.

Kendra thought for a moment. "No. Just my gym shorts and T-shirt and socks."

"What about you, Madison? Do you keep your gym stuff in a gym bag or backpack?" Nancy asked.

"Um, I keep my stuff in a gym bag," Madison replied.

"Have you checked it lately?" Nancy asked.

Madison shook her head. "Nope. My mom usually goes through my gym bag between classes and washes everything."

Nancy stood up. "Then we all need to go over to your house right away," she announced.

The Clue Crew, the Klue Krew, Nadine, and Violet filed down the stairs to the Foleys' basement. "There's a clean pile of your laundry on top of the drier, Madison!" her mother called after her from the kitchen.

"Thanks, Mom!" Madison shouted. "I still don't know why we're looking through my laundry," she grumbled to Nancy.

"You'll see," Nancy said with a smile.

The Foleys had a finished basement with a Ping-Pong table, a pool table, and lots of comfy-looking chairs in front of a large plasma-screen TV set. The washer and drier were in a smaller room to the right of the main room. There, Madison pointed to a pile of clothes.

"Nancy Drew, you're leading us on a WGC," Deirdre complained. "In case you don't know, WGC stands for wild goose chase."

Nancy didn't reply. She walked over to the

pile of clothes on the drier. She started pick-
ing through the items one by one. There were a
couple of tops. There were three pairs of jeans.
There were some socks and underwear, too.

At the very bottom of the pile was a pair of
gym shorts and a gym T-shirt.

And under those items . . . was a pink hoodie!

Nancy checked out the label carefully. It said
"Design by Lula" on it. It also had the initials
NN—for Nadine Nardo.

"Ta-da!" Nancy said, holding the hoodie up for everyone to see.

Nadine grabbed it from her. "Is that my hoodie? Oh my gosh, it is!" She started jumping up and down.

"Nancy, how did you know it was here?" Violet asked her.

"Violet told us that she took Nadine's hoodie out of her locker on Tuesday, in the middle of gym class, so she could check it out," Nancy began. "But she didn't put it back. She left it on the floor, on a messy pile of clothes. Madison had the locker next to Nadine's, and she accidentally put Nadine's hoodie in her gym bag along with her other stuff. But she didn't know it was there because her mom cleaned out her gym bag when she did the laundry."

"That is so complicated," Violet said. "You must be pretty awesome detectives to have figured that out!"

"They are!" Nadine said. She gave Nancy a hug. She hugged George and Bess, too.

"The Clue Crew with C's solved the case!" she exclaimed. "Yay!"

Deirdre stepped forward. "Actually, that's not exactly right. The Klue Krew with K's solved the case. After all, your hoodie was in Madison's house."

Everyone cracked up—even Madison and Kendra. "Nice try, Deirdre," Nadine giggled. "The Clue Crew with C's wins the contest!"

"Well, being a detective is kind of dumb, any-way," Deirdre grumbled. "It's way too much work!"

Bess leaned over to Nancy and George. "Does that mean the Klue Krew with K's is going to stop being a detective club?" she whispered.

"Sounds like it," Nancy said. "Maybe they'll give us their trench coats and magnifying glasses, since they won't be using them anymore!"

Be Your Own Fashion Designer with This Super-Cool T-shirt Project!

Have you ever wanted to create your own awesome T-shirt design? It's easier than you think. Here's how!

You Will Need:

An old towel or other padding

1 T-shirt in a plain solid color. (If it's brand-new, make sure you or your parents wash and dry it first, *without* using fabric softener.)

1 piece of cardboard cut to fit inside the T-shirt

A piece of paper and colored pencils, crayons, or markers

Various rubber stamps with shapes. (You can find these in discount stores, craft stores, and other stores, too. Choose letters, numbers, stars, moons, flowers, bugs, birds—whatever looks fun!)

Fabric paint in various colors

A few paintbrushes with fine tips. (You will use these to spread paint onto the rubber stamps, and also to decorate the T-shirts freehand.)

Get Ready to Make Some Wearable Art!

❀ Lay the T-shirt on top of a lightly padded surface. An old towel works really well!

❀ Put the cardboard inside the T-shirt. This will keep the fabric paint from seeping through and making every-thing really yucky!

❀ Using the paper and colored pencils, crayons, or markers, sketch a design for your T-shirt. First draw a picture of the T-shirt. Then take a look at your rubber stamps and see what kinds of shapes you have to play with. Do you want to design a row of pretty yellow daisies and pink butterflies? Or spell your name over and over in red, white, and blue? Use your imagination—and go crazy!

❀ Now put your design on the T-shirt! Decide which stamp shape and color you'll use first. Using a paintbrush, paint a layer of fabric paint onto the stamp. Carefully press the stamp down on the fabric. Don't press too hard, and don't wiggle the stamp back and forth. Just as carefully, lift the stamp. When done, wash the stamp and try another color!

❀ Repeat the previous step as many times as necessary until your design is completed. You can also use a paintbrush to add your own touches freehand (like brown dots in the middle of your daisies, or purple stripes on your butterflies' wings; always clean the brush before you change colors).

❀ With your T-shirt lying flat, let your design dry completely, following the instructions on the fabric paint packaging.

One Last Thing: When you (or your parents) wash your T-shirt for the first time, it's best to turn it inside out and wash it in cold water. It's also best to dry your T-shirt on the lowest setting, or just let it hang dry.

For even more fun, invite your friends to bring a plain T-shirt to your next party—and design T-shirts together! Nancy, George, and Bess love to do this!

Turn the page for a sneak peek at

Nancy Drew

and the CLUE CREW

 #22 Unicorn Uproar

The girls raced to the fence. The unicorn stood at the far end of the pen, too far away for them to get a good look.

"My mom said there would be a unicorn here at the fair," George said. "But I thought she was joking!"

"That's no joke," Bess said, staring over the fence at the unicorn. "That's got to be for real."

Until now Nancy had seen unicorns only in books and as stuffed animals in toy stores. But the unicorn inside the pen looked pretty for-real to her.

"The sign says his name is Sparkle," Nancy pointed out.

"Probably because his horn sparkles in the sun!" Bess declared.

A woman dressed in a red cape and feathered cap shouted as she walked by: "Lords and ladies, boys and girls! Come one, come all to ye royal parade!"

"Let's go," Nancy said. She stuck her wand into the back pocket of her jeans. Then she ran with Bess and George to catch the parade.

"Bye, Sparkle," Bess called back. "See you later!"

A crowd had already gathered on the field for the parade. Nancy, Bess, and George squeezed to the front just in time to see marching knights, jugglers, and the king and queen waving from a castle float.

When Nancy spotted Enchanted Elly marching in the parade, she remembered her magic wand. But when she glanced back at her pocket, it was gone.

"Bess, George!" Nancy cried. "I think I lost my wand!"

"Maybe it really was magic," Bess gasped. "And it magically disappeared!"

George shook her head and said, "Or maybe it just fell out of your pocket on the way here."

The girls left the parade to retrace their steps. As they neared Sparkle's pen, Nancy spotted a flash of silver in the grass. As they ran closer, the glittery purple star and lavender ribbons came into view.

Nancy smiled with relief as she picked up the wand. "See, Bess?" she said happily. "It didn't disappear."

But Bess wasn't looking at the wand. She was staring into the unicorn pen.

"You guys . . . what happened to Sparkle?" Bess asked.

"What do you mean?" Nancy asked. She looked into Sparkle's pen too. But instead of seeing the white unicorn she saw Rex Martindale. His hands were on his hips as he spoke loudly to a teenage boy.

"Seth, as Sparkle's handler you should know where he is!" Rex was saying.

"I told you, Rex," Seth said. "When I got back to the pen, Sparkle was gone."

Nancy, Bess, and George traded stunned looks.

"Did he say Sparkle was gone?" Nancy whispered. "As in . . . missing?"